LONGMAN

Pride
and
Prejudice

Jane Austen

Simplified by John Turvey

Longman

Longman Group UK Limited,
Longman House, Burnt Mill, Harlow,
Essex CM20 2JE, England
and Associated Companies throughout the world.

First published in 1991

ISBN 0-582-03045-5

Set in 10/13 point Linotron 202 Versailles
Produced by Longman Group (FE) Limited
Printed in Hong Kong

Acknowledgements

'Photographs © BBC' 1980.

The cover background is a wallpaper design called NUAGE,
courtesy of Osborne and Little plc.

Stage 4: 1800 word vocabulary

Please look under *New words* at the back of this book
for explanations of words outside this stage.

Contents

Introduction

1	A new neighbour	1
2	The dance and after	4
3	Mrs Bennet's good idea	8
4	A visitor	13
5	Mr Wickham	16
6	The dance at Netherfield	22
7	Mr Collins makes an offer	25
8	Disappointments	30
9	At Rosings	35
10	Mr Darcy speaks	42
11	Lydia's wish	50
12	Derbyshire	54
13	A wedding	60
14	A return	64
15	An unexpected visit	66

Questions   71

New words   74

Introduction

Pride and Prejudice is the story of a young man and a girl. He is proud – although attracted to her, he thinks himself too good for the girl and her family. She is prejudiced – having once formed an opinion of him, she refuses to change it.

A lot of the book is about marriage: about marrying for true love, or false love, or money, or safety, or rank or because other people expect it. It is also about how people make marriages and live together in families, and how people should and should not behave to each other.

But the main point about *Pride and Prejudice* is that it is very funny. There are not many books like this in which all the jokes are as easy to understand now as when they were written nearly two hundred years ago. This is because the people Jane Austen laughs at can be found in every time and place.

Even as a child, Jane Austen was known in her family for imitating people, the way they spoke, the way they looked. She wrote little plays, and also enjoyed acting with her family and friends. In summer they put on plays in a wooden building in the garden, and in winter in the dining-room. Her books are full of imitations. Imitations of silly people saying silly things in their own special ways. In this book Mrs Bennet, Mr Collins and Lady Catherine are good examples.

Jane Austen was born in 1775 in a small village in the south of England. Her father was, like Mr Collins in this book, the village parson. However, unlike Mr Collins he was a man of character and intelligence who passed on his education to all his seven children.

Jane, the youngest, learnt French and some Italian. She sang and played the piano and was good at needle-work. But above all she read a great deal of English literature.

She started writing herself as a child, and in 1796 finished her first book, which, when re-written some years later, was to become *Pride and Prejudice*. Her father, who always encouraged her writing, tried to have it printed, but without success. In fact, it was not until 1811 that her first book was printed, and two years after that *Pride and Prejudice* in its final form appeared. Altogether she completed six books before she died in 1817.

To understand the world of *Pride and Prejudice* we need to understand the world in which its writer lived. Southern England in her time was a land of small farms worked by labourers who in turn worked for farmers. These farmers often did not own their farms, but paid rent four times a year to the landowners. These, the gentle-men, lived in large houses surrounded by parks, or open grassland with a few trees here and there and perhaps a lake to make them more beautiful. Some, like Mr Bennet in this story, would live comfortably without being very rich. Others might own many farms, and have a house in London and a noble title. But as long as they owned land they had a position in society and were considered gentle-men. Some were interested in books or in making their houses and land beautiful. But most of them lived for country sports, hunting and shooting.

Village churches and their parsons were supported by a special tax, and some parsons lived very comfortable lives. Since landowners often had the right to give the job of village parson to whoever they wished, they usually chose someone who suited them, sometimes a younger son. Thus in this book Mr Collins was the right kind of person for Lady Catherine. On the other hand, Darcy did not think Wickham would be a suitable person to be a parson. In all cases, however, parsons were educated people and considered to be of the class of gentlemen. The Austens, although they had very little money, were of this class, and it was about this class and its world that Jane Austen wrote.

It was a small world. She travelled little, met few interesting people, and nothing very unusual happened to her. She did not marry, and lived with her family in the village where she was born until her father's death in 1805, then in the towns of Bath and Southampton, and finally in a village again with her mother and only sister.

However, this does not mean that nothing of interest was going on in the world around her. For a large part of her life England was at war with France. The French husband of a cousin whom she knew well had his head cut off in 1789. Two of her brothers were officers in the navy and reached high rank in the wars. The country life she lived was not as quiet and peaceful as the life she describes in her books. Nor did people behave quite as politely as they do there.

In other words, in her books she made her own world, which was not exactly the world around her. But that, after all, is what the best writers do.

Chapter 1
A new neighbour

It is a well-known fact that a single man with plenty of money must be in need of a wife. *He* may not know this, but neighbours with unmarried daughters are quite sure of it. So imagine the arrival in a neighbourhood of a man who is single, rich and young. Imagine its effect on Mrs Bennet, who has four unmarried daughters.

"My dear Mr Bennet," she said one day, "Netherfield Hall has been let at last."

Mr Bennet continued to read his newspaper.

"Don't you want to know who's taken it?"

"You're determined to tell me, and I'm ready to hear you," he said.

"Well, then, it's been taken by a rich young man called Bingley," she said excitedly.

"Is he married or single?"

"Why single, my dear, and with £5,000 a year. What a fine thing for our girls."

"Indeed, and how can it affect them?"

"My dear Mr Bennet, how can you be so annoying? You must know that I'm hoping he'll marry one of them."

"Is that his intention in settling here?"

"Intention? Nonsense," exclaimed his wife. "But it's surely quite likely that he may fall in love with one of them, and so you must visit him."

Mr Bennet returned to his paper. "I don't see the need. You and the girls can go. I'll write him a note to say that I agree to his marrying whichever of the girls he chooses. Though perhaps I ought to recommend Elizabeth to him. They are all silly girls, but she has a little more sense than her sisters."

Mrs Bennet complained that it was impossible for her to call on a single gentleman. But her husband would not agree to visit Mr Bingley. He was a strange mixture of clever jokes and long silences. Even after twenty-three years of marriage she did not understand him or his jokes. But, then, she was not as clever or educated as him. She was also easily upset. Her one aim in life was to find husbands for her daughters – Jane, Elizabeth, Catherine and Lydia. Her pleasures were visiting, talking and clothes.

Mr Bennet was one of the first to visit Mr Bingley the next morning. He had always intended to go, but he had been determined not to tell his wife. Nor did he tell her after his return. But as he sat with his family that evening he talked continually of dances, of Mr Bingley, of introductions. At last his wife could bear it no longer.

"I'm tired of Mr Bingley! I don't ever want to hear his name again," she said.

"I'm sorry to hear that," her husband replied. "But why didn't you tell me before? If I'd known this morning I wouldn't have called on him. But since I have, we can't now escape knowing him."

Mrs Bennet's joy can be imagined. But her husband did not stay to observe it. Nor could she find out from him what Mr Bingley was like. For this, annoying though it was, she had to go to her friend and neighbour, Lady Lucas. From her she learnt that he was good-looking, charming and fond of dancing. And that was not all. He planned to attend the next public dance in the nearby town of Meryton with a party of family and friends.

Mr and Mrs Bennet

Chapter 2
The dance and after

The Bennets were not rich, but they lived comfortably with servants at Longbourn, their house in the country. Mr Bennet received £2,000 a year in rent from his land, and his wife had a little money of her own.

However, their situation was worse than it seemed because of a lawyer's agreement, made years before by Mr Bennet's grandfather. Since Mr Bennet had no son, the property, when he died, would pass to a distant cousin. His daughters would have nothing unless they married. This explains the great hopes of Mrs Bennet.

So when Bingley left for London she was alarmed. Was he not coming to the dance, then? Her friend, Lady Lucas, calmed her. He had only gone, she said, to gather a party for the dance. The next report was that he was bringing twelve ladies – bad news for the ladies of Meryton. But he finally arrived at the dance with only four other people: his two sisters, the husband of one of them, a Mr Hurst – and another gentleman.

Mr Bingley was certainly good-looking and very friendly. But his companion, Mr Darcy, attracted more attention. He was not only better-looking, but also (so people said) had £10,000 a year. At first people admired him. But then they noticed he was proud. He danced once with each of Bingley's sisters, but showed no interest in any other ladies.

How different from Mr Bingley who danced every dance and made himself popular with everybody – and in particular with Mrs Bennet. For he danced with her eldest daughter, Jane, not just once, but twice.

Her sister, Elizabeth, was not so lucky. Because there were not enough gentlemen she had to sit down for two dances. During this time Mr Bingley left the dance-floor to speak to Darcy, who was standing near.

"Why aren't you dancing?" he asked. "I've never seen so many attractive girls in all my life."

"You're already dancing with the only really attractive one," Darcy replied, looking towards Jane.

"That may be true," said Bingley, "but one of her sisters sitting just behind you is also very pretty."

Darcy turned. "Bearable," he said, "but why should I dance with a girl nobody else wants to dance with?"

When his family arrived home, Mr Bennet had to listen to his wife describing every lady's dress and who Mr Bingley had danced with dance by dance. "If only," he said, "he'd broken his leg in the first dance!"

But Mrs Bennet just had to mention Mr Darcy. "You should have seen him standing there alone, thinking himself so important. 'Bearable', indeed!"

Next morning, Jane expressed her surprise at Bingley asking her to dance a second time.

"It was no surprise to me, since you were by far the prettiest girl in the room," replied Elizabeth. "He seems very pleasant. You've liked worse men."

"Dear Lizzy, you shouldn't say such things."

"It's true," said Elizabeth. "You have such good sense, but you don't seem to see people's faults. Do you like his sisters?"

"They're very pleasant, when you talk to them."

Elizabeth *had* talked to them, and did not agree.

They were fashionable London ladies who could be charming when they liked. But they were proud. They

5

looked down on the country society of Meryton.

A week later Elizabeth talked about Jane to Charlotte Lucas, her closest friend. Mr Bingley's admiration for Jane was growing. Jane liked him too. But as usual she hid her feelings under the same cheerful friendliness which she showed to everyone.

"A woman may often want to hide her feelings for a man," said Charlotte, "to stop people talking. But if she hides them too well, she'll lose him."

"But Mr Bingley must see that Jane likes him."

"He doesn't know her like you. She should try harder to attract him. Then, when she's sure of him, there'll be time enough to fall in love with him."

"That may be a good plan for a girl who only wants to get married," Elizabeth said. "But Jane isn't like that. She'd never marry somebody she didn't love. Just now she doesn't know him, or her own feelings."

"I don't think one *can* know a man before marriage, and it's better that way. If people knew all about the person they were going to marry, they wouldn't do it."

"You say that," said Elizabeth, laughing, "but you know you'd never act like that yourself."

But while Elizabeth was twenty, Charlotte was twenty-eight, and like her friend had little money to expect from her family. Also she was not so pretty. She sometimes felt she was getting too old to find a husband.

From that time Elizabeth watched her sister and Mr Bingley closely. Perhaps because of this she hardly noticed that someone was watching her. But one evening at a party at the Lucas's house it became quite clear. Whoever she spoke to, Mr Darcy was always near.

"What does he mean by listening to my conversation?" she said to Charlotte. "If he continues, I'll let him

6

know what I think. He's listening for things he can make jokes about with Mr Bingley's sisters."

The truth was different. As Darcy saw more of Elizabeth, his ideas began to change: she might not be exactly beautiful, but she had nice eyes. As for her conversation, it was not like fashionable London talk. But there was something very attractive in her easy, laughing manner. Later that evening, as he was talking to Sir William Lucas, she happened to pass by.

"Miss Eliza," said Sir William to Elizabeth, "you're not dancing. Mr Darcy, you can't refuse." He took her hand to give to Darcy. He, though surprised, was very willing to take it. But she pulled it away.

"Please, Sir William," she said. "I don't want to dance. Mr Darcy is only being polite."

"This is hardly politeness," Sir William said, "for who would refuse a chance to dance with Miss Bennet?"

Elizabeth smiled as she remembered another time and moved away. Sir William also walked off leaving Darcy looking thoughtful. Just then Miss Bingley came up. "I think I can guess what you are thinking," she said. "You're thinking how unpleasant it would be to spend many evenings in this kind of company."

"You're quite wrong," said Darcy. "I was actually thinking how attractive a certain young woman is."

"Indeed?" said Miss Bingley in a softer voice. She smiled and looked into his eyes. "And who is she?"

"Miss Elizabeth Bennet."

"Miss Elizabeth Bennet? I'm astonished. How long has she been a favourite? When's the wedding to be?"

"That's exactly what I expected you to say," said Darcy. "A lady's thoughts jump straight from admiration to love, and from love to marriage."

Chapter 3
Mrs Bennet's good idea

One morning a few days later, a servant arrived at Long-bourn with a letter for Jane.

"Well, Jane, who's it from? What's it about? Tell us, my dear," cried Mrs Bennet impatiently.

"It's from Miss Bingley," Jane replied. "The gentlemen are going out to dinner with the officers from the regiment that has its camp at Meryton, and she asks if I can have dinner with her and her sister. Can I take the carriage?"

"No, my dear," said her mother, who was disappointed that Jane would not see Mr Bingley. "You'd better take a horse. It seems quite likely to rain, and then they'd have to ask you to stay the night." Jane did not like this idea, or the reason for it. But since her father said that the carriage horses were needed on the land that day, she had to go on horseback.

In fact, Mrs Bennet's plan succeeded all too well. Soon after Jane left it began to rain so heavily that she arrived quite wet. It went on all the evening and she did not return. But when next morning a note arrived to say that she was ill in bed, Mrs Bennet's plan did not seem so clever. Elizabeth was worried and decided to walk to Netherfield to find out how she was, even though her mother was against it.

"What will they think when you arrive with mud on your shoes and stockings?" she cried.

When she arrived at Netherfield the whole company, except for her sister, were still at breakfast. Bingley's sisters received her politely, but she felt that they looked

down on her for walking across muddy fields. Her shoes and stockings *were* dirty, and her hair was blown by the wind. But the exercise had given life and colour to her face, and the gentlemen noticed this, and not the dirty shoes.

Jane was not well, and did not improve during the morning. So Elizabeth was grateful when Mr Bingley asked her to spend the night at Netherfield too. After dinner, as soon as she went up to sit by Jane, Bingley's sisters began to talk about her: about her manners, her conversation, her ideas, her clothes – none of which pleased the ladies of Netherfield. Only Jane, among all the Bennets, was good enough to praise.

"She's a very sweet girl," said Mrs Hurst, "and I wish with all my heart she could find a good husband. But with such a family and no money there's little chance of it. Her mother has no sense at all."

"You should meet the uncle and aunt in Meryton," laughed Miss Bingley.

"And they've another uncle who's a merchant in London," said Mrs Hurst.

"If they had twenty uncles like that, it wouldn't make the Miss Bennets any less attractive," said Bingley, who was not happy with this talk.

"True," said Darcy, "but it must still make it more difficult for them to marry men of good position in the world." Bingley was silent, but his sisters continued to amuse themselves with their friend's relations for some time.

Later that evening while Darcy was writing a letter, Miss Bingley was trying to make him talk to her.

"How happy your sister will be to receive a letter from

Elizabeth walks to Netherfield in the rain

you!" she said. But Darcy went on writing.

"How very fast you write!"

"You're mistaken. I write very slowly."

"Please tell your sister that I long to see her."

"You asked me before, and I've already done so."

Just then Elizabeth entered the room. She had thought it only polite to join the company, and not sit with her sister all the time.

"Miss Eliza Bennet," said Miss Bingley as soon as she appeared, "let's take a walk to the window. We can see if it's still raining."

Elizabeth was surprised by this show of friendship, but after they had walked up and down several times she understood the reason. Miss Bingley was trying to attract Darcy's attention – and he did look up. Though who could say whether his eye was caught by Miss Bingley or Miss Bennet. In any case, it was enough for Miss Bingley to invite him to join them.

But he shook his head and said: "There can only be two reasons for walking up and down like that. It's better if I stay here."

"What can he mean?" Miss Bingley said.

"Why, he means to laugh at us," said Elizabeth, "and the best way to prevent him is not to ask what he means." But Miss Bingley had to ask, for she could not disappoint Darcy in anything.

"You're walking up and down," Darcy explained, "either because you have secrets to discuss, or because you want me to admire you. But if the first is true, you can't really want me; and if the second is true, I can see you much better from here."

"Oh!" cried Miss Bingley. "How shall we punish him for such a speech?"

"Surely it's easy for someone like you who knows all his faults," said Elizabeth. "Laugh at him."

"Mr Darcy has no faults. He's not to be laughed at."

"Not to be laughed at! That's a very unusual advantage, and I hope it remains unusual. I wouldn't want to know many people like that," said Elizabeth.

"Miss Bingley's too kind," said Darcy. "I have my faults. I only try to avoid the foolish ones."

"Such as pride?" Elizabeth asked.

"Pride *may* be a fault in someone who has nothing to be proud about," he said.

Elizabeth smiled. Turning to Miss Bingley she said: "If pride is no fault, he has no faults."

"But I have," said Darcy. "For example, I find it hard to forgive people once I lose my good opinion of them. My dislikes are strong. That's surely a fault."

"Hatred *is* a fault. Oh, yes. Hatred is a good fault to choose. I can't laugh at that."

"Everyone has some fault like that," said Darcy.

"And yours, you say, is a readiness to hate people."

"And yours is wanting to misunderstand them. Or might I call it prejudice?"

At this point Miss Bingley grew tired of a conversation which she was not sharing in. "Let's have some music," she said, moving to the piano. Darcy followed her. He began to feel the danger of paying too much attention to Miss Elizabeth Bennet.

The next day Jane was a little better. Although both Mr Bingley and her mother wanted her to stay, she decided to go home. Elizabeth agreed. Both for the ladies of Netherfield and for herself the visit had been long enough.

Chapter 4
A visitor

Some days later, while the Bennet family was having breakfast, Mr Bennet produced another little surprise.

"I hope," he said to his wife, "you've planned a good dinner today, as I'm expecting a guest."

"Who do you mean, my dear? I don't expect anybody today – unless perhaps Charlotte Lucas stays. And I know my dinners are better than any she has at home."

"The person I mean is a gentleman, and I've never seen him before in my life." This news produced all the excitement that Mr Bennet had hoped for.

"Some weeks ago I received a letter from my cousin, Mr Collins, who, as you know, will become the owner of Longbourn when I die."

"Oh, that man!" cried Mrs Bennet. "I can't bear to hear his name. Why does the law allow him to do this to us?" She continued her loud complaints on this favourite subject of hers for some time, while her daughters tried to calm her.

"If you'll allow me to read this," said Mr Bennet, "you may learn why he's coming." He read aloud:

Hunsford, Kent

Dear Sir,

The quarrel between you and my father has always caused me unhappiness; and since his death I have often wished to end it. You will be pleased to hear that I have now made up my mind. Last Easter I became a parson and was appointed by the noble and honourable Lady Catherine de Bourgh to the care of this village. As a parson, I think it is my duty to spread peace. Therefore I hope that the question of Longbourn will not make you refuse my offer of friendship. I am deeply sorry that I will one day have to take over the home of your respected daughters. I apologise to them, and hope I may reduce this harm – but of this I will speak later. If you are willing, I shall present myself to your family on Monday next at four o'clock. I should like to stay twelve days as Lady Catherine has most kindly allowed me to be absent for this time. I remain, Dear Sir, your friend.

William Collins

"So we can expect this man of peace at four," said Mr Bennet. "He may become a friend – if his Lady Catherine is kind enough to let him come again."

Elizabeth wondered what he meant by "reducing the harm". And why he apologised because Longbourn would pass to him? "It's not his fault – and if he could prevent it, he wouldn't. Do you think he can be a very sensible man?"

"I don't, my dear," said her father. "He seems an interesting mixture: humble and self-important at the same time. I quite look forward to meeting him."

To the younger Bennets the only interesting visitors were young officers from the camp near Meryton – not parsons. But Mrs Bennet's hatred of Longbourn's future owner suddenly and strangely seemed to disappear.

Mr Collins arrived exactly on time. He was a tall, serious, heavy-looking young man of twenty-five, with the manners of someone much older. He talked continuously to Mrs Bennet, praising everything he saw, from her daughters to the dining-room furniture. Only when he praised the house itself was she upset. She could not forget that one day it would all be his.

During dinner Mr Bennet said little. There was no need, for Mr Collins had much to say. But when later they all returned to the sitting room he asked his guest about Lady Catherine and her house, Rosings.

This was a subject Mr Collins was ready to talk about all night: how she had already asked him to dinner twice, *and* sent for him to be the fourth person at a game of cards; how she had planned shelves for his upstairs cupboards, and advised him to get married.

"Does she have any family?" asked Mrs Bennet.

"One daughter – with a great deal of property."

"Ah!" cried Mrs Bennet. "Then she's luckier than many girls. What's she like? Is she beautiful?"

Mr Collins gave some thought to his answer. "She's a most charming young lady. Lady Catherine herself says that Miss de Bourgh has more *real* beauty than other girls, because she looks more truly noble. She's not, however, in good health and her education has suffered. But she's perfectly polite.

"It's sad that her health prevents her from mixing in society. As I told Lady Catherine myself, the world of fashion has lost one of its brightest jewels – I like to make little remarks like this. They please the ladies, and it is a duty I owe to Lady Catherine."

"Quite right," said Mr Bennet. "How lucky to have this skill. Do these remarks suddenly enter your mind? Or do you think of them before?"

"I think of them before, but try to make them sound natural when I bring them out," said Mr Collins.

Mr Bennet was fully satisfied. His cousin was even more foolish than he had hoped.

15

Chapter 5
Mr Wickham

Any advice of Lady Catherine to Mr Collins was a command. He *had* to get married, and that was why he had come to Longbourn. He had heard that his cousins were pretty girls, and had come to marry one of them. Nor did he change his mind when he saw them, and by the end of his first evening he had decided on Jane. But Mrs Bennet made him think again. She approved his marrying one of her daughters. But she had to warn him – Jane might soon be marrying someone else.

In the time it took for Mrs Bennet to put a log on the fire, Mr Collins's feelings flew from Jane to Elizabeth. Elizabeth, he thought, might be acceptable.

That morning the girls decided to take Mr Collins to visit their mother's sister, Mrs Philips, in Meryton. This plan was strongly supported by Mr Bennet, who had been troubled by Mr Collins's company since breakfast.

When they reached the town Lydia and Catherine looked up and down for somebody they knew. They did not have to wait long. The attention of all four girls was soon caught by two young men across the road. One was a young officer called Denny that they already knew. The other, not in uniform, was a stranger, and unusually good-looking. Pretending to be interested in a shop window, Lydia crossed the road and placed herself in their path. In this way they all met Mr Denny's friend, who was about to join the army.

This friend, Mr Wickham, was as charming as he was good-looking, and they all stood there talking for some time. It was such a pleasant conversation that they did

Wickham talks to Elizabeth

not at first hear the sound of horses. It was Bingley and Darcy riding towards them. When they stopped, Bingley explained that they had been on their way to Longbourn to invite them to a dance at Netherfield.

But Elizabeth was not listening. She was watching Darcy, and was very much surprised by what she saw. As soon as he saw the stranger his face turned white. Mr Wickham seemed equally unhappy at this meeting. The two gentlemen raised their hats to each other, but neither said a word. Clearly they had met before.

The two horsemen soon rode on, and the rest of them walked along to the house of Mr Philips. Lydia tried hard to persuade the two young men to come inside, but Mr Denny had duties at the camp, and they walked on.

While Mrs Philips and Mr Collins exchanged polite words, Lydia waited impatiently. She wanted to know more about Mr Wickham. But although her aunt knew most of what happened in Meryton, she could not tell them any more about this gentleman. However, she said that several of the officers were coming to dine the next evening. If the party from Longbourn would come too, she would also invite Mr Wickham.

As they walked home, Elizabeth told Jane what she noticed when Darcy and Wickham had met. But Jane could not explain it. It was a mystery.

The next evening, after Mr Collins's long apologies for leaving his hosts alone, he and his cousins drove off to the Philips's house at Meryton.

Mr Collins looked round. The room, he said, was quite like the small summer breakfast room at Rosings. This did not at first sound like praise to Mrs Philips. But Mr Collins was kind enough to tell her more about Lady

Catherine's house, and she began to understand that Mr Collins was doing her a great honour.

As soon as the other gentlemen came in with Mr Philips, Elizabeth knew she had not been wrong to admire Mr Wickham. His looks, his manners, his conversation put him far above the other officers. Here at last, unlike Darcy, was a true gentleman.

When the card tables were put up, he preferred to sit with Lydia and Elizabeth. At first Lydia took all his attention, for she was a talker like her mother. But she also liked cards, and at last she went over to the tables, leaving Wickham alone with her sister.

Elizabeth knew she could not introduce the interesting subject of the meeting with Darcy in Meryton. So it was lucky that Mr Wickham began by asking how long Darcy had been at Netherfield.

"About a month," she replied. "I believe he has a fine house and a great deal of land in Derbyshire."

"He has – and nobody could tell you more about Pemberley and the Darcys than me. I've known that house and family all my life. So you may wonder," he went on, after seeing her surprise, "at the unfriendly meeting we had yesterday. Do you know him well?"

"As well as I shall ever want to. I don't think he has a pleasant character," said Elizabeth.

"I've known him too long to be able to judge him fairly. But many people would disagree with you. They're easily influenced by money and rank."

"Not in this neighbourhood. Nobody likes him here."

"I wonder," said Wickham, after a pause, "how long he's likely to stay."

"I've heard nothing about his leaving. But I hope your plans won't be changed by his being here."

"I shan't be driven away by him. He has more reason for avoiding me since he's treated me very badly. But I shan't say a word against him. I still have too much respect for his father – one of the best of men."

Mr Wickham began to talk of other things, but soon returned to Darcy. "I'm a disappointed man. I wasn't brought up for the army but for the Church. Old Mr Darcy promised me a good position in the Church. But when he died and this position became free, his son gave it to someone else."

"But how could he act so badly?" cried Elizabeth.

"He's jealous. You see, my father looked after old Mr Darcy's property, and I was brought up and educated with the son. Perhaps I was too much of a favourite of the old man. I think his son has never forgiven me."

Elizabeth remembered Darcy's words at Netherfield about his unforgiving character. "What sort of girl is his sister?" she asked.

Mr Wickham shook his head. "It makes me sad to speak badly of any Darcy, but she's like her brother – good-looking, but very proud. I used to play with her when she was a child, but she looks down on me now."

"I'm surprised by his friendship with Mr Bingley. Surely he must know what sort of man Mr Darcy is."

"Perhaps not. Mr Darcy can be charming when he likes – especially to those he thinks are his equals."

Just then the card party began to break up, and Elizabeth asked Mr Collins how he'd done. He replied that he had lost every game. "But I don't mind. I don't have to worry about the loss of five shillings – thanks to the goodness of Lady Catherine de Bourgh."

Wickham looked up at the sound of that name. Later, taking Elizabeth aside, he asked how her cousin was connected with that lady, and she explained.

"You may not know," he said, "that Lady Catherine is Mr Darcy's aunt. Her daughter will be very rich. It's thought that she and Mr Darcy will marry, and so bring together two large properties."

Elizabeth smiled to think of Miss Bingley's hopes.

Next morning Elizabeth told Jane what she had learnt about Darcy. Her sister was surprised. She could not believe that Bingley would choose the kind of friend described by Wickham. She did not know what to think.

"I know exactly what to think," said Elizabeth. "I know the kind of man that Mr Darcy is."

However, a more important matter was now arising. The day of the Netherfield dance was near, and the entire Bennet family (except, of course, its head) was in a state of excitement. Elizabeth, full of happy thoughts of dancing half the evening with Wickham, asked Mr Collins if he was going to the dance.

"I'm not one of those who think parsons should never attend a dance – especially when it's given by a gentleman of good character like Mr Bingley," he said. "I hope for the honour of dancing with all my cousins. Indeed, I would like to take this opportunity of asking for the pleasure of the first two dances with you."

Elizabeth was speechless. She had quite expected Mr Wickham to ask her for just these dances – and to have Mr Collins instead! But there was no escape.

Worse followed. Rain kept the Bennets inside for days. So she was prevented from seeing more of Wickham. Worse still, it was becoming clear that Mr Collins was taking an uncomfortably close interest in her. Surely, he ... but, no, that was impossible.

Chapter 6
The dance at Netherfield

Elizabeth dressed carefully for the dance. For this was the night when she must win Mr Wickham's heart.

But all her hopes depended on one thing – that Wickham would be there. So imagine her feelings on entering the room and finding he was not. Had Darcy persuaded his friend not to invite him? Later she learnt from Lydia that this was not so. Wickham had left for London on business (he had told his friends). But she knew the real cause of his absence was Darcy.

However, anger against Darcy was soon replaced by feelings of a different kind. Mr Collins was coming to claim her for his dances. He was no dancer, and what followed was misery. It was hard to say which was worse: the many times that he trod on her foot, or the apologies that followed. But the dance ended at last, and she ran to Charlotte to tell her all her troubles.

But she had hardly begun, when another gentleman came to ask her to dance – Darcy. She was too surprised to refuse. For some time they stood silent on the dance-floor, waiting for the music to begin. Elizabeth made some remark to which Darcy replied. Then the dance started and there was more silence.

"It's your turn to say something now, Mr Darcy," she said. "I talked about the dance. You could talk about the size of the room or the number of dancers."

"I'll say whatever you want me to say," he replied.

"That reply will do for the moment. Perhaps later I may say that private dances are pleasanter than public ones. But for the moment we can be silent."

So they remained silent, until Darcy asked if she often walked to Meryton.

"Quite often. When you met us the other day we had just been making a new friend," Elizabeth replied.

"Mr Wickham is always able to make friends," he said coldly. "But he doesn't find it so easy to keep them."

"He's been unlucky enough to lose your friendship, and is likely to suffer for it all his life," she said.

The dance ended. Both dancers felt glad not to have to continue the conversation. Darcy led her to a seat next to Miss Bingley, and went off in anger: but anger that was more against Wickham than Elizabeth.

"So, Miss Eliza," said Miss Bingley, "your sister has been asking me about George Wickham. I hear you're quite delighted with him. But you may not know that his father was old Mr Darcy's servant. Let me warn you, as a friend, not to believe everything he says. He has harmed Mr Darcy. I don't know how, but I do know that Mr Darcy cannot bear to hear his name. I pity you, Miss Eliza. You'll find out your favourite's true character in the end."

"So far as I understand you, Mr Wickham's only fault is that his father worked for old Mr Darcy," said Elizabeth coldly.

"I beg your pardon," said Miss Bingley as she got up and walked away. "I was only trying to be kind."

"Insulting girl," said Elizabeth to herself. "She knows nothing, but believes everything Darcy says."

But now a very excited Mr Collins was coming towards her. Surely he could not want another dance?

"I've made a most important discovery," he cried. "In this very room tonight is a close relative of Lady Catherine. I must offer him my respects at once."

"You're surely not going to introduce yourself to Mr Darcy?" Elizabeth cried.

"Indeed I am. I believe him to be Lady Catherine's nephew. It's my duty to introduce myself, and tell him that she was quite well two weeks ago yesterday."

Elizabeth tried hard to stop him, but without success. She knew that Darcy would not encourage it.

She could not hear what Mr Collins said. She only saw the expression on Darcy's face become more and more distant. The meeting ended with a short bow from Mr Darcy and he moved away. "I have no reason to be dissatisfied," said Mr Collins, as he returned rubbing his hands. "Mr Darcy received me most politely."

It was at supper, however, that Elizabeth's most painful experience took place. She had been avoiding her mother all evening so as not to hear her talking. But now she found herself seated between her mother and Lady Lucas, with Darcy not far away.

Mrs Bennet could only talk of one thing – her hopes of Jane's marriage to Bingley. She never got tired of repeating its advantages: that Mr Bingley was so rich; that Bingley's sisters loved Jane so much, and that the younger daughters might meet other rich men.

Elizabeth knew that Darcy could hear this, but it was useless to try to make her mother speak more quietly.

"What's Mr Darcy to me?" she thought. "We owe him nothing." But even Mrs Bennet stopped talking at last, and Lady Lucas found comfort in some cold chicken.

Mrs Bennet returned home happily certain that in three months Jane would be settled at Netherfield. She was equally sure that her second daughter would soon be Mrs Collins. But she did not care so much about this. For Elizabeth was her least favourite child.

Chapter 7
Mr Collins makes an offer

The next day Mr Collins asked Elizabeth to marry him. After breakfast he found her with her mother and Catherine at their needlework. "I hope, Madam," he said to Mrs Bennet, "that you will not mind my speaking to your daughter Elizabeth in private."

"Oh dear – yes, certainly – I'm sure Lizzy will be very happy – come, Catherine, I need you upstairs," said Mrs Bennet, picking up her pins and needles.

"Mother, please don't go – I'm sure anything Mr Collins has to say can be heard by anybody," said Elizabeth.

"Nonsense, Lizzy. I want you to stay and hear Mr Collins," said her mother, and left the room.

"Believe me, my dear Miss Elizabeth," Mr Collins began, "your modesty only adds to your charm. Without this show of unwillingness you would be less attractive to me. But let me put your mind at rest. Your mother has given her permission for this little talk. The subject of it can be no secret to you. Almost as soon as I arrived here, I chose you as the companion of my future life. But before I let my feelings run away with me, let me give my reasons for getting married."

He then went on to do this. First he thought it right for a parson to set a good example. Secondly he thought marriage would add to his happiness. Thirdly, and most important of all, Lady Catherine advised it.

"A gentleman like you, Mr Collins, should marry," she had said. "Choose carefully. Choose a lady for my sake – and for your own sake choose an active, useful sort of person. Bring her to Hunsford, and I will visit her."

Mr Collins said he was sure Elizabeth would suit Lady Catherine perfectly. For she would surely treat the great lady with the respect which her high rank deserved.

"Now," he said, "it only remains for me to express the full strength of my feelings for you. I care nothing for money, since I know that you have none – except, of course, for the £1,000 at four per cent which will be yours when your mother dies. Be sure that I shall never say a word of complaint about this when we're married ..."

Elizabeth had to interrupt him at this point. "You forget, Sir, that I haven't yet given you an answer. Let me do so now. I'm greatly honoured by your offer, but I'm afraid it's impossible for me to accept it."

Mr Collins was not in the least discouraged. "I know young ladies very often refuse offers of marriage which they intend to accept later," he said.

"If there really are young ladies like that," said Elizabeth, "I'm not that kind of young lady. The truth is that we could never make each other happy."

"When I next speak to you on this subject," he said, "I'm sure I shall receive a different answer."

"Surely, Mr Collins, I have made my answer clear enough," said Elizabeth.

"I still prefer to think that your refusal, dear cousin, is not serious. My reason is that I have so much to offer: my position in life, my connection with the de Bourgh family. After all, having so little money, you may not receive any other offer of marriage. I cannot really think you will refuse me in the end."

Elizabeth could do no more to change Mr Collins's beliefs, so she left him. Mrs Bennet, who had not been far away, now came in to give him her best wishes. Mr Collins was still sure of his success, but when Mrs Bennet heard what her daughter had said, she was not so satisfied, and said: "She is a silly girl. She will not listen to other people who know best."

"If she *is* that sort of girl," said Mr Collins, "perhaps she would not do for Lady Catherine."

"Don't worry, Mr Collins. She is only silly sometimes. Leave her to me," replied Mrs Bennet, and she went straight to Mr Bennet's library.

"Oh, Mr Bennet," she said, "we are all in confusion. You must come and make Lizzy marry Mr Collins. She says she won't have *him*, and he may change his mind and not have *her*."

Mr Bennet remained calm. He sent for Elizabeth and said: "I understand that Mr Collins has made you an offer of marriage and you have refused it." Elizabeth agreed. "And your mother says you must accept him."

"Yes," cried Mrs Bennet, "or I'll never speak to her again."

"Well," said Mr Bennet, "you have a hard choice. If you refuse Mr Collins, your mother won't speak to you. If you accept him, I shan't speak to you."

Elizabeth smiled. She would not have to marry Mr Collins. But her mother was disappointed. During the next few days she continued to threaten or persuade.

The problem was what to do with Mr Collins. He was determined not to return to Hunsford before the day planned, and Elizabeth found it uncomfortable to talk to him. However, help was near. Charlotte was kind enough to sit and listen to him, and he seemed glad of her attention. Elizabeth was grateful.

But she did not know that Charlotte had her own reasons for behaving as she did.

On the last day of his stay, before anyone else was up,

Mr Collins left Longbourn and walked to the Lucas's house. Charlotte saw him coming and hurried out to meet him, as if by accident, in the lane. This time there were no long speeches. Charlotte was ready to accept his offer of marriage. Her parents agreed, and Mr Collins was back at Longbourn before midday.

The Bennets had noticed his absence, but received no explanation, even when he left for home the next day. However, when Mrs Bennet said she hoped to see him again at Longbourn, he surprised them. He said he would like to come and stay again very soon. Mr Bennet, who did not wish for such a quick return, asked if he thought Lady Catherine would let him leave Hunsford again. But Mr Collins did not seem to think this a difficulty, and after long speeches of thanks, drove off.

Mrs Bennet at first thought he was planning to return to make an offer to one of the younger girls. But later that day Charlotte came to tell Elizabeth her news, followed a little later by her father.

Elizabeth was upset. How could Charlotte accept a man like Mr Collins? But for Mrs Bennet it was worse. Now she had to listen to Lady Lucas talking all the time about the coming marriage of her daughter. Even worse was the thought of Charlotte taking her place at Longbourn after the death of Mr Bennet. However, her husband had a word of comfort for her.

"Let's hope for better things, my dear," he said. "Perhaps you may die before me."

Mr Collins asks Charlotte to marry him

Chapter 8
Disappointments

If Elizabeth was upset by Charlotte's marriage, Jane was much more upset by events at Netherfield. Soon after the dance, Bingley had to go to London. Then Jane received a letter from Caroline Bingley. She said her brother's business was taking longer than expected. She and her sister had left Netherfield to join him.

This was bad news. But a second letter brought worse. The Bingleys would not return that year. She said her brother was sorry he had not had time to see his friends before he left. She also mentioned Darcy's sister. She clearly hoped Bingley would marry her.

It was some days before Jane showed this letter to her sister. "I'll forget him in the end," she said. "There is nothing to blame him for. If I imagined stronger feelings on his side, the fault is mine."

"The fault is *not* yours," said Elizabeth angrily.

"Please, Lizzy," said Jane. "You only hurt me more by blaming him. You can't expect a lively young man to be always so careful of other people's feelings."

"I don't accuse Bingley of trying to deceive you – only of weakness. He's too much influenced by his sister and Mr Darcy. She wants him to marry Miss Darcy. Also Miss Bingley wants to marry Mr Darcy. She thinks one marriage may lead to another. She followed her brother to London to persuade him not to return."

Elizabeth did not go on. She knew it was painful. But their mother never stopped talking about it.

Mr Bennet treated the matter lightly. "So, Lizzy," he said, "your sister is disappointed in love, I hear. But she mustn't worry. It makes a girl interesting to her friends. Perhaps you could arrange for the same to happen to you. There are enough officers in town to disappoint every girl in the country. Wickham could be *your* man. He would disappoint you admirably."

In fact, Wickham tried to make Jane feel better. Everything he had told Elizabeth about Darcy before, he now told to the others. It was his opinion that Darcy was the real cause of Jane's disappointment.

Help also came from Mrs Bennet's brother and his wife who arrived as usual to spend Christmas with them. Mr Gardiner, the London merchant, was an educated man, quite different from his sister. His wife, too, was a sensible woman who had always been close to Jane and Elizabeth. After describing the latest London fashions, she had to listen to all their troubles.

"I don't blame Jane," said Mrs Bennet, "for she would have got Mr Bingley if she could. But Lizzy! It makes me mad to think she might have been Mrs Collins by now. The result is that the Lucas's, who always think of themselves before anybody else, will now have a daughter married before me. But I'm very glad to hear what you say about long sleeves."

Later, alone with Elizabeth, Mrs Gardiner said: "I'm sorry for Jane, but these things do happen. Poor girl, she's easily hurt. Do you think it would help her to come back with us and stay in London for a while? However, she mustn't think she's likely to see this young man. We live in a very different part of town, and we don't know the same people."

"So much the better," said Elizabeth, even though she could not quite think that Bingley's love was dead.

"She may feel she has to call on the sister, though."

"Miss Bingley will break off their friendship," Elizabeth replied.

That week among the daily guests at dinner the most regular was Mr Wickham. Mrs Gardiner could not help noticing how much he and Elizabeth were together.

"You're too sensible, Lizzy, to fall in love simply because someone warns you against it," she said. "So I'm not afraid of asking you to be careful. I've nothing to say against Mr Wickham, who seems an interesting young man. And if he had money, I don't think you could do better. But two people without money would not make a good marriage."

"My dear Aunt, you're being very serious."

"Yes, and I hope you'll be serious too."

"Well, then, have no fear. At present I'm not in love with him. But he is by far the most attractive man I've ever met. And where there's love, you know, young people are rarely held back by lack of money. How can I promise to be wiser than the rest? But, yes, I'll be careful."

Soon after Jane and the Gardiners departed for London, Charlotte and Mr Collins were married. Before she left, Charlotte asked Elizabeth to come and stay with her in the spring. Elizabeth did not refuse, but she did not expect pleasure from a stay with Mr Collins.

Letters came from Jane in London. She had called on Caroline Bingley. But it was four weeks before Miss Bingley called on her. The visit was short, and the visitor's manner made it clear that their friendship would not be continued. Even Jane could no longer avoid seeing Miss Bingley's true character. Jane's unhappiness was plain, and Elizabeth was worried.

Meanwhile, Wickham's interest in Elizabeth had become less. He now admired another girl. The reason for his admiration was the £10,000 that had just come to her from her grandfather. But Elizabeth refused to be upset by this. She knew he would have chosen *her* if she had had £10,000. It was natural for a young man like him to marry money and obtain independence, she said. She did not stop to think how different her opinion of Charlotte in the same situation had been.

March came, and the visit to Hunsford was talked of again. By then Elizabeth felt quite ready to see Charlotte again, even though Sir William and Maria, Charlotte's sister, would also be going. She would have to listen to their empty conversation in the carriage. But they would spend a night in London at her uncle's, and so she would see Jane.

Jane seemed pleased to see them, although their aunt said that she was often very unhappy. Mrs Gardiner also found time to speak to Elizabeth about Wickham.

"I'd be sorry if he was only interested in money," she said. "He paid this girl no attention before."

"If she doesn't mind his attentions, why should we? A man without money can't always behave as we might wish. I'm tired of polite young men. Thank heaven I'm going tomorrow to stay with Mr Collins! In the end stupid men are the only ones worth knowing."

"Take care, Lizzy," said her aunt. "That sounds like disappointment." But seeing that her niece was upset, she said that Mr Gardiner was planning a trip to the Lakes in the summer. Would she like to join them? She accepted with delight. To see the Lakes had for long been the dream of her life.

Next day Hunsford appeared just as it had been de-scribed. Mr Collins immediately took them on a tour of the house. As he spoke, Elizabeth felt he was directing his remarks particularly at her. Perhaps he wished her to feel what she had lost by refusing him.

At dinner, Rosings was the main subject of his talk. "On Sunday you'll have the honour of seeing Lady Catherine at church," he said. "I needn't say that you'll be delighted with her manners. She behaves quite charming-ly to my dear Charlotte."

Next morning Elizabeth was in her room when she heard Maria calling excitedly outside her door. "Oh, my dear Eliza, do come to the window! There's such a sight to be seen."

She followed her and saw two ladies in a light carriage talking to the Collinses at the garden gate.

"Is this all?" cried Elizabeth. "I expected at least that the pigs had got into the garden. Who are they?"

"Why," said Maria, "it must be Miss de Bourgh and Mrs Jenkinson who looks after her. Just look at her. I didn't expect her to be so thin and pale."

"She's very rude to keep Charlotte out in this cold wind. Why doesn't she come in?"

"Oh, Charlotte says she hardly ever does. It's a great honour when she comes in," said Maria.

Elizabeth began to think about this unhealthy girl with her bad-tempered look. Yes, she would make the perfect wife for Mr Darcy.

At last the carriage moved on, and Mr Collins came in, rubbing his hands delightedly. "We're all invited to din-ner at Rosings tomorrow," he said. "Who could have expected such attention as this so soon after your arrival? This is true de Bourgh politeness."

Chapter 9
At Rosings

All next day Mr Collins could talk of nothing but Rosings. "Don't worry too much about your dress," he said. "Lady Catherine will not think badly of you for being plainly dressed. She likes to see a difference in clothes between the different ranks of society."

Even when the ladies had all gone to their rooms, he came several times to their doors telling them to hurry. Lady Catherine did not like to be kept waiting. The result was that Maria arrived at the great house in a state of terror, and even her father felt nervous.

They passed through the entrance hall, where Mr Collins unnecessarily pointed out the high ceiling and several large statues. They then followed the servants through a smaller room to an enormous sitting room, where Lady de Bourgh, her daughter and Mrs Jenkinson were sitting.

Their hostess was a tall, large woman with a face of strong character. She did little to make her visitors feel at home or to forget their lower place in society. She spoke as someone who knew she was right. And every remark showed a strong belief in her own importance. Wickham's description had been just right.

Her daughter was quite different. She seemed without character. She spoke little, and when she did, had nothing interesting to say.

Dinner was very grand with all the servants and silver plates that Mr Collins had promised. He sat at the end of the table opposite Lady Catherine, and loudly praised every dish as soon as it appeared.

Elizabeth wondered how Lady Catherine could bear so

much praise. But this was something she never got tired of. There was little real conversation. Mrs Jenkinson spent all her time trying to make Miss de Bourgh eat, Maria was still too frightened to speak, and Sir William only repeated Mr Collins's praises.

When the ladies left the gentlemen and went back to the sitting room, there was nothing to do but listen to Lady Catherine talk. This she did without stopping, giving her opinions and advice about everything.

At last she turned her attention to Elizabeth. How many sisters did she have? How old were they? Were they likely to get married? Were they good-looking? Where had they been educated? What carriage did their father keep? Elizabeth felt the impoliteness of her questions, but answered without showing her feelings.

Lady Catherine was not at all satisfied with the education of the Bennet girls. "No teacher? How was that possible? Four daughters brought up at home without a teacher? I never heard of such a thing. Who taught you, then? Who attended to you?"

"We were always encouraged to read," replied Elizabeth, "and those who chose to be lazy were lazy."

"Yes, no doubt, but that's what a teacher is meant to prevent. If I'd known your mother, I would have strongly advised her to get one. It's remarkable how many families I have helped in this way. I've placed four nieces of Mrs Jenkinson in good families. Mr Collins, did I tell you Lady Metcalf called yesterday to thank me? She finds Miss Pope a treasure. 'Lady Catherine,' she said, 'you've given me a treasure.'"

When the gentlemen joined the ladies again, the company sat down to play cards. At Elizabeth's table little was said. But at the other table their hostess was again

Lady Catherine de Bourgh

talking most of the time – mainly about the other players' mistakes. Mr Collins was talking for the rest of the time – agreeing with Lady Catherine, thanking her for every point he won, and apologising if he won too many. Sir William still said little. He was too busy storing his mind with things to remember about life at Rosings, so he could tell his family.

When the de Bourghs were tired of playing cards, a carriage was ordered, and their guests were sent away.

In the carriage Elizabeth was asked by Mr Collins about their evening. For Charlotte's sake she tried to make it appear more enjoyable than it had really been. But even this did not satisfy him, and he continued to talk about Lady Catherine's politeness until bedtime.

Sir William left after a week, and the Collinses and their remaining guests settled down to the quiet country life of Hunsford. Mr Collins spent much of his time gardening, and when Miss de Bourgh drove by, he would call out excitedly to the others.

Sometimes Lady Catherine herself called. During these visits she would ask what they were doing, advise them to do it differently, try to re-arrange the furniture or scold the maid. Further invitations to Rosings gave Elizabeth little pleasure, but she found life otherwise quite pleasant.

Just before Easter she learnt that Lady Catherine was expecting guests – her nephews, Mr Darcy and a Colonel Fitzwilliam. It would be interesting to see Darcy with Miss de Bourgh. It would show if Wickham was right about the plan for them to marry.

The visitors' arrival was reported by Mr Collins, who had spent all morning walking in the lane in order to bow to their carriage when it appeared. The next day he hurried off to Rosings, eager to show his respect.

An hour later Charlotte looked out of the window and was astonished to see him returning with both Lady Catherine's visitors.

"I must thank *you* for this, Eliza," she said. "Mr Darcy would not have come so soon to visit *me*."

Colonel Fitzwilliam was the younger son of a lord: a man of about thirty, not good-looking, but in every way a gentleman. He talked easily and pleasantly, and so made up for the silence of his cousin, though Darcy did ask Elizabeth about her family. In answering she mentioned that her sister was in London, and asked if he had seen her. She noticed that he looked a little confused as he said he had not.

Two days later they were invited to Rosings. It was noticeable that they were not as welcome as before, when they were the only company; and Lady Catherine talked most of the time to Darcy. Fitzwilliam, though, was glad to see them. Life at Rosings was dull for him. He much preferred to talk to Mrs Collins's pretty friend. Indeed, they talked with such spirit that at last his aunt turned round.

"What's that you're saying, Fitzwilliam?" she said. "What are you talking of? What are you telling Miss Bennet? Let me hear what it is?"

"We're talking of music, Madam," the Colonel said.

"Of music! Then speak louder. It's my greatest delight. I must share in the talk if you're speaking of music. There can be few people who enjoy music more than me. How is Georgiana getting on, Darcy?"

Darcy replied that his sister was making progress.

"Tell her from me, she cannot hope to be good unless

she practises a great deal. I've told Miss Bennet this several times. She's welcome to come here every day and play on the piano in Mrs Jenkinson's room. She would be in no one's way in that part of the house."

Darcy looked ashamed at this remark, and his aunt went on to other subjects. But when later Elizabeth began to play, he drew away from the others and sat down behind her.

"You're trying to frighten me, Mr Darcy, by coming over to hear me play," she said.

"Frighten you? I think you sometimes enjoy stating opinions that you do not hold," he said.

Elizabeth laughed, and said to Fitzwilliam: "Your cousin means that you shouldn't believe a word I say. How unlucky to meet someone who uncovers my real character here, where I'd hoped to be believed. But it's unwise of you to do so, Mr Darcy. I may say things about you that will shock your relatives."

"Tell me more," said Fitzwilliam. "I'd like to know how he behaves among strangers."

"You shall, then. But be prepared for something bad. I first met your cousin at a dance. And at this dance do you know what he did? He only danced twice, although there were more ladies than men."

"I didn't know any ladies there," said Darcy.

"Of course, nobody can be introduced at a dance."

"I don't find it easy to talk to strangers."

"Shall we ask the reason for this?" said Elizabeth.

Fitzwilliam smiled. "He won't try," he said.

Elizabeth went on: "If I don't play the piano well isn't it because I don't practise enough?"

"All right," said Darcy, laughing. "I understand. Bring me young ladies and I'll practise to please you."

During the evening Elizabeth several times observed Darcy's manner towards Miss de Bourgh. He gave no sign of any loving interest in her. She began to think that Miss Bingley did not yet need to give up hope.

Next morning Elizabeth was alone in the house writing a letter when the door-bell rang. Thinking it might be Lady Catherine, she put the letter away to avoid her questions. But it was Darcy, alone, who appeared.

He seemed as surprised as her, saying he thought the other ladies were also in. He then sat down, and there was a short conversation followed by silence. At last he began to talk about the Collinses, and said how lucky Charlotte was to be so near her family.

"Near?" said Elizabeth. "It's almost fifty miles."

"What's fifty miles of good road? Only half a day's journey."

"I still wouldn't say that Charlotte was settled near her family."

"I suppose," continued Darcy, "that you wouldn't like to live so far from Longbourn."

Elizabeth could not understand where this conversation was leading, but was saved from making a reply by the return of Charlotte and Maria. Darcy stayed a few more minutes then left.

"What does this mean?" asked Charlotte as soon as he was gone. "My dear Eliza, he must be in love with you, or he would never have called like this."

But when Elizabeth told her of his silences, she agreed that it was not very likely. However, Darcy continued to make visits, though always with his cousin. Fitzwilliam, attracted by Elizabeth, clearly enjoyed these occasions. But why did Darcy come?

Chapter 10
Mr Darcy speaks

One day, as Elizabeth was walking in the park of Rosings as she often did, she heard footsteps behind her. She looked round and was glad to see not Darcy, as she had feared, but Colonel Fitzwilliam.

"So, are you leaving on Saturday?" she asked.

"Yes – if Darcy doesn't change his mind again. He arranges things just as it pleases him."

"I don't know anybody who enjoys pleasing himself more than Mr Darcy," said Elizabeth.

"Don't we all, when we can," replied Fitzwilliam. "It's just easier to do it when, like him, one is rich. We who are poor have to do what other people want."

Elizabeth laughed. "Surely the sons of lords need not suffer too much. Seriously, does lack of money really prevent you from doing what you want?"

"Not in small things. In bigger ones younger sons *may* suffer. They cannot always marry who they like."

"Unless they like rich women – which they often do."

"Men in my rank of society," said Fitzwilliam, "can't often afford to marry without some thought of money."

"Is this," thought Elizabeth, "meant for me?" Not wanting him to think she was affected by his remark, she laughed and went on: "But if your cousin needs someone to give orders to, I'm surprised *he* doesn't marry. He does, though, have a sister. As she is under his care he can tell her to do what he wants."

"Ah, but you're wrong," said Fitzwilliam. "He has to share the care of his sister with me. His father left both Darcy and myself in charge of her."

"And does she give you much trouble? Young ladies of her age are not always easy to control. If she is a true Darcy she, too, may like to please herself."

As she spoke, Elizabeth saw Fitzwilliam looking at her quite seriously. She realised that by accident she had come too close to the truth. "But I'm sure she's charming," she continued. "She seems a great favourite of some ladies I know, Mrs Hurst and Miss Bingley."

"Their brother is a great friend of Darcy."

"Oh, yes," said Elizabeth, "Mr Darcy is a great friend of Mr Bingley, and takes good care of him."

"Why, yes," said Fitzwilliam. "From something Darcy said, I think he really does take care of him."

"What do you mean?"

"I hear he saved Bingley from an unwise marriage."

Elizabeth was silent. Then she said: "Why should your cousin decide what's good for his friend? We can only suppose Mr Bingley was not very deeply in love."

"That's quite possible," replied Fitzwilliam, "but it would make my cousin's success seem much less."

Her companion left her at the house with much to think about. Now she knew it was Darcy who had destroyed her sister's hopes rather than Miss Bingley. Jane herself could not have been the reason for Darcy's action. It was his own pride. He could not allow his friend to marry into a family which he looked down on.

These thoughts brought on a headache. She could not go with her cousins to tea at Rosings.

Alone in the house later that evening, she heard the door-bell ring. To her amazement Darcy walked in. After rather hurriedly asking her how she felt, he started walking up and down the room. Then, turning suddenly, he said in a voice that he could hardly control: "I've struggled against my feelings, but it's no use. I have to tell you that I love you."

Elizabeth's astonishment was now complete. She could only sit there helplessly while Darcy asked her to marry him. He spoke well, but not in a way that was likely to persuade her. He spoke of his feelings about her family not being equal to his. He said a lot about how he had tried to fight against his love for her. He spoke, too, of his anxiety, but Elizabeth saw no signs of this. He did not seem to expect a refusal.

When he had finished she said: "It's usual to thank gentlemen who come with an offer of marriage, for it's a great honour to a lady. But in this case I don't think I can. I've never asked for your love, and you don't really want to give it to me. I'm sorry to cause unhappiness to anyone, and I can only hope that yours will not last long."

Darcy leant back against the fire-place. His face was pale with anger. For some moments he could not speak. At last he said: "Is that your only reply? Or am I not allowed to know why you refuse me?"

"I might equally well ask," said Elizabeth, "why you chose to insult me by saying that you love me against your will. But I have other reasons. You know I have. Even if I *had* loved you, do you think I would have accepted the man who had ruined my sister's happiness? You know you separated her from Mr Bingley."

She paused to see the effect of her words, but he showed no signs of shame or sorrow.

"I've no wish to deny it. I can only say that I've been kinder to my friend than I've been to myself."

"But this is not all. Long before I knew what you'd done to my sister I knew what you'd done to Mr Wickham. Can you deny that you've destroyed his life?"

"You take a strong interest in that gentleman's affairs," said Darcy, less calmly than before.

"Anyone who knows about his misfortunes can't help taking an interest in him."

"His misfortunes!" said Darcy with a bitter laugh. "Oh, yes, his misfortunes have been great indeed. And this is your opinion of me. I could have pretended just to love you without saying anything else. But I hate to hide my feelings, and I'm not ashamed of them. Could you expect me to feel pleased with your relations, whose rank in life is so much below my own?"

Elizabeth had to control her anger: "There was no way in which you could have made me accept you. From our first meeting I was struck by your pride, your self-importance, your carelessness about the feelings of others. From the very beginning I was quite sure you were the last man on earth I should want to marry."

"You've said enough," said Darcy. "I understand your feelings for me, and can only be ashamed of the feelings I have for you." With those words he left.

Elizabeth cried for half an hour. Her astonishment, however, went on growing. She could not understand how she had affected Darcy in this way. Next day she woke still feeling upset. After breakfast she went for a walk round the edge of the park, not wanting to meet anyone. But as she stopped by the gate Darcy appeared, holding a letter, which he put into her hands. He bowed, and left her, while she opened it then and there with shaking hands and read:

Do not be afraid that I shall repeat the offer I made last night. I neither want to upset you, nor to appear foolish. My hopes are best forgotten. But since you

45

made certain remarks about my actions and character, you must let me answer them.

You accuse me of two things: first, that I separated Mr Bingley and your sister without any thought of their feelings; secondly, and worse, that I was unjust to Mr Wickham. I hope, when I have explained, you will no longer blame me for either. But if I hurt you again, I can only say that I must be honest.

I saw from the first that Bingley was attracted to your sister. But it was only at the Netherfield dance that I understood how far things had gone. A remark of Sir William Lucas showed me that everyone expected them to marry. I also failed to notice in your sister any signs of love for my friend. Perhaps I was wrong; but although she seemed to enjoy my friend's company, she did not seem to love him.

There were other reasons why I acted as I did. Your family's position in society is one. This did not seem to worry my friend as much as it worried me. But also – it hurts me to say this – I often found the manners of your mother, your younger sisters, and sometimes even your father, hard to accept.

After my friend left for London, I talked with his sisters. Finding that we thought alike, we decided to follow him. There I pointed out the disadvantages of marrying your sister. These did not influence him. But when I told him my opinion of your sister's feelings, he decided not to return to Netherfield.

I do not know what Mr Wickham has accused me of. So I had better explain that his father was an honest man who served my father well. Because my father had a good opinion of the son, he gave him a gentleman's education, intending him to enter the

Church. But I was of the same age, and knew him better. I could see that he was bad from the beginning.

When my father died he left Mr Wickham £1,000, and asked me to give him a good position in the Church, as soon as one became free. But Mr Wickham did not think he was suited to the Church, and I agreed. He suggested I should give him money to study law instead, and I agreed to this, too. He went off to London, where he spent the money on wild living. Then, two years later he came to me, asking for that place in the Church. I refused, and he became insulting. I did not see him again until last summer in Meryton.

There is something else you should know about Mr Wickham, but this must be a secret. When my father died, he left my sister in the care of Fitzwilliam and myself. About a year ago we took her away from school and settled her in my London house. We employed a certain Mrs Young to look after her. However, we did not know that this lady had once known Mr Wickham. He soon became a visitor, and with Mrs Young's help set out to make my sister fall in love with him. Having known her as a child, it was not too difficult for a man like him to persuade her to run away with him. Luckily I found out in time.

Mr Wickham's main aim was, of course, my sister's money. But revenge must also have been in his mind.

This is the story of my dealings with Mr Wickham. If you doubt it, you may approach Colonel Fitzwilliam who will tell you the same.

Fitzwilliam Darcy

Darcy gives Elizabeth the letter

Elizabeth read this letter with increasing amazement. She did not believe he had thought her sister was not in love with Bingley. And his other reasons for breaking up their friendship made her angry. He showed no regret for anything he had done.

But when he spoke of Wickham, her feelings became confused. She wanted to disbelieve him, but as she re-read the letter it became more and more difficult to blame him. True, he gave no proof of his accusations against Wickham, but neither could she prove him wrong. She tried to remember examples of Wickham's good deeds or kind words, but could only remember good manners.

When she read about Darcy's sister, she remembered her conversation with Fitzwilliam. She remembered, too, how Wickham had boasted that he would not be driven away from the Netherfield dance by Darcy. Yet he had allowed this to happen. Also, it was only after Darcy and the Bingleys left Netherfield that Wickham had started to spread his stories about Darcy widely.

As for Darcy, though all agreed that he was proud, only Wickham had ever said he was unjust. Elizabeth began to feel shame. She had always been proud of her judgement of character, and had blamed her sister for only seeing the good. But who had been more blind?

Thinking of Jane made her return to the letter. At least, this part of his explanation could not be believed. But on re-reading it she again felt unsure. Charlotte, too, had seen what Darcy described. Jane did not show her feelings openly. As for the remarks about her family, these hurt. But could she deny them?

Thinking these thoughts, she walked for two hours before returning home. There she learnt that Darcy and his cousin had called to say goodbye, but could not stay.

Chapter 11
Lydia's wish

The gentlemen left the next morning, and Mr Collins and his guests dined at Rosings that same day.

"Those two young men were very sorry to leave," Lady Catherine said. "I thought Darcy seemed particularly sad. He gets more and more fond of Rosings."

Mr Collins was quick to suggest that Miss de Bourgh might have some part in Darcy's fondness for Rosings. This remark was well received by mother and daughter alike. Elizabeth was wondering. Suppose she had accepted Darcy's offer. How would Lady Catherine de Bourgh have received the news? Not with great joy, she thought.

She had re-read his letter till she knew every word. When she studied the expression of his thoughts, she was angry with him. When she studied the thoughts themselves, she was angry with herself. For he was often right. Her younger sisters did behave badly. Her father would not control them, and her mother did not even see the need. They were uneducated, lazy and only interested in their appearance.

At last came the end of their stay at Hunsford. Lady Catherine wished them a good journey and invited them back to stay with the Collinses next year. Miss de Bourgh held out a pale, thin hand for them to shake.

"It seems only a few days since we arrived," said Maria, as their carriage drove off next morning. "Yet how many things have happened!"

"A good many, indeed," replied Elizabeth sighing.

"We've dined nine times at Rosings, besides having

tea three times. What a lot I'll have to tell!''

"And I," thought Elizabeth, "what a lot to hide!"

Two days later Elizabeth, Maria and Jane left London. As they entered the town where Mr Bennet's carriage was waiting for them, they saw Lydia and Catherine looking out of the window of an inn. The sisters proudly showed them a table set out with a cold lunch. "This is a surprise," said Catherine. "We're paying for you all."

"But you must lend us the money," added Lydia, "as we've just spent ours on these hats. They're not very nice, but it won't matter much what we wear this summer since the regiment is leaving in two weeks for Brighton, and I do so want Papa to take us there for the summer. It would probably hardly cost anything."

"We have some other news for you," Lydia went on. "About a person we all like – dear Wickham. There's no danger of his marrying that girl after all. She's gone to her uncle's in Liverpool. Wickham is safe."

"I'm sure he never cared three pence for her," said Catherine, "the nasty, spotty little creature."

"I was hoping one of *you* might find a husband before getting back," said Lydia. "Jane will soon be too old. I'd be ashamed of not being married at twenty-three."

As soon as they had settled down after the excitement of coming home again, Elizabeth told Jane about Darcy's offer of marriage. She repeated everything he had said about Wickham, but felt she could not mention Bingley. It would be more than Jane could bear.

Even Mrs Bennet never mentioned Bingley to Jane. "Well, Lizzy," she said, "what's your opinion of this sad business of Jane's? For my part I'm determined never to speak of it again to anybody. I told my sister Philips so the other day. He's a very unkind young man, and I don't suppose there's the least chance of her getting him now."

"I don't believe he'll ever come again."

"Well, it's for him to choose. Nobody wants him to come. The only good thing is that Jane may die of a broken heart, and then he'll be sorry."

But Jane's sorrows were soon equalled by those of Lydia and Catherine. For these were the last days of the regiment's stay in Meryton.

"What's to become of us! What are we to do!" they exclaimed. "How can you go about smiling, Lizzy?"

Their loving mother shared their sorrows. She remembered how she had suffered twenty-five years before. "I'm sure I cried for two whole days when Colonel Miller's regiment went away."

"If only we could go to Brighton!" cried Catherine.

"If only!" said Lydia. "But Papa is so cruel."

But there was a sudden end to Lydia's sorrows. Mrs Forster, the young, recently married wife of the regiment's colonel, asked her to stay in Brighton with her. She had always found Lydia good company.

Lydia's joy, her mother's delight and Catherine's jealousy cannot be described. As for Elizabeth, she felt her father ought to stop the plan. Brighton was not safe for a wild girl like Lydia, and Mrs Forster was not the sort of woman who would protect her.

But Mr Bennet only said: "Lydia will never be happy until she's made a fool of herself somewhere. Isn't it better that she should do it in Brighton rather than in Meryton?"

"But what Lydia does, Catherine imitates. Don't you see how their behaviour harms Jane and myself?"

"Whoever knows you and Jane," said Mr Bennet, "cannot think badly of you for having two silly sisters. We'll have no peace if Lydia doesn't go to Brighton, so let her go. Colonel Forster is a sensible man and will keep her out of real trouble. Besides, at Brighton the officers will have better women to talk to." Elizabeth was not persuaded, but she could say no more.

On the regiment's last night Wickham dined at Longbourn. He had not sat with Elizabeth since her return, and he asked about Hunsford. When she said she had met Fitzwilliam, he looked alarmed. The Colonel, he said, was very different from Darcy.

"Very different – but I think Mr Darcy improves."

"You mean his manners. I dare not hope that his true character has improved," said Wickham.

"Oh, no," said Elizabeth, "his true character, I believe, is very much unchanged."

Wickham looked doubtful.

She added: "I mean that the more one knows him, the better one understands him."

Wickham by now looked definitely unhappy. He said very little more to Elizabeth that evening.

After Lydia and the regiment went, life became much duller. There were fewer parties. Catherine remained dissatisfied, and Jane was still unhappy. Elizabeth thought more and more about her trip to the Lakes.

However, two weeks before they were due to depart a letter arrived. Mr Gardiner had a lot of business. There would not be enough time to go to the Lakes, so they had decided to go to Derbyshire. This was a disappointment. But Derbyshire was very beautiful. It also had many fine houses – including Pemberley. But that, of course, was not a house she cared to see.

Chapter 12
Derbyshire

In August, the Gardiners collected Elizabeth and drove on to Derbyshire, where they spent several very happy weeks. They travelled about visiting great houses, beautiful rivers and attractive old towns.

One evening, while planning the next day's journey at their inn, Mrs Gardiner remarked that Pemberley was not far away. "Wouldn't you like to see a house you've heard so much about?" she asked. "They say the grounds are delightful."

Elizabeth did not say yes or no. She would quite like to go, but dared not risk seeing Darcy. But next morning she talked to the maid and learnt that he was not at present living there. So she agreed to go.

They entered the park, and after driving for some time through beautiful woods, came out on to higher ground. There, across the valley, on the far side of a lake, was the great house. It would be something, thought Elizabeth, to be mistress of Pemberley.

As the housekeeper, a pleasant, elderly woman, showed them round, Elizabeth could not help comparing it with Rosings. There, everything was for show. Here was a house to live in.

Darcy, they were told again, was away, but was expected the next day with a large party of friends. What an escape! To have missed him by one day!

Meanwhile they had stopped in front of some family pictures. "And that," said the woman, "is my master."

"It's a very fine picture," said Mr Gardiner. "But, Lizzy, you can tell us whether it's like him or not."

The housekeeper's respect for Elizabeth increased. "Does the young lady know Mr Darcy?" she asked.

"A little," Elizabeth said.

The housekeeper needed no more encouragement to talk about her master, and how she wished he would spend more time at Pemberley. "If only he would get married! But I don't know who's good enough for him."

Mrs Gardiner smiled, but the housekeeper shook her head. "I say no more than the truth, and anybody who knows him will say the same. I've never heard an angry word from him, and I've known him since he was four."

This was amazing. But she had more to say: about his gifts to the poor, his fairness to the farmers who rented his land and his kindness to his sister.

"This account of him is quite different from that of your friend," whispered Mrs Gardiner.

When they had seen the house, they were handed over to a gardener who was to show them the grounds. As they walked away, Elizabeth stopped to admire the fine front of the house.

Then, from round a corner suddenly appeared its owner.

It was impossible to avoid him. Their eyes met, and they stood there, completely still. Darcy was the first to move. He came forward and spoke – not with perfect control, but with perfect politeness. She hardly dared lift her eyes to his face. She was so ashamed at being found there. At last Darcy seemed to have nothing else to say, and after a moment's silence made his excuses and walked away.

The Gardiners had recognised Darcy from his picture, and expressed their admiration. But Elizabeth was not listening. Why had she come here? It was the worst thing

Darcy and Elizabeth meet in the gardens at Pemberley

in the world. Did it not look as if she was throwing herself at him? He must have only just arrived. If only they had left five minutes earlier!

As they walked by the lake her thoughts were still of Darcy. How his behaviour had changed! No longer his old stiff manners, but true politeness. She did not understand. What was now passing through *his* mind? In spite of her refusal was it possible he might still have some feeling for her?

As they turned back at the end of the lake they saw Darcy again approaching. When he asked Elizabeth to introduce him to her friends, she smiled to herself. Darcy was about to learn that a London merchant might still be a gentleman and man of education. She had *some* relations she did not have to feel ashamed of.

When Mrs Gardiner felt tired and took her husband's arm, Darcy and Elizabeth walked on ahead. She could not wait to explain that she had thought he was away. He explained that, having so many guests to prepare for, he had thought it better to return a day earlier. Among these guests were Bingley and his sisters. He also asked if he could introduce his sister to her.

She refused his invitation to enter the house, and they stood talking until the others appeared. There was much that she wanted to say, but so many subjects seemed forbidden.

"I was surprised," said Mrs Gardiner, as they drove away. "He has perfect manners. I wonder how you came to think him so unpleasant?"

Elizabeth had agreed that Darcy should bring his sister to call on the day after she arrived. She was surprised, therefore, to see their carriage appear outside the inn the very next morning. He could not even wait a day.

Her aunt and uncle were amazed. They could no longer explain it in any other way. Mr Darcy must be in love with their niece.

When Miss Darcy arrived, Elizabeth was surprised to see that she was even less at ease than herself. Georgiana Darcy was tall, quite pretty, not at all proud, but clearly unused to company. She could only with difficulty be made to talk.

Bingley also came, as friendly as before. His behaviour to Georgiana did not suggest that his sisters' hopes of a marriage were likely to come true. This did not prove that he still had some feeling for Jane. But he did, when the others were talking among themselves, ask how she was in a serious voice.

After the visit she did not have to fear curious questions from her uncle and aunt. Could she even have answered them? How did she feel about Darcy? She had stopped hating him long ago. She was ashamed of having hated him. More than that she did not know.

That evening Mrs Gardiner remarked that Miss Darcy's call should be returned the next day. Only one thing made Elizabeth uncomfortable. Caroline Bingley would be there. She would not welcome her at Pemberley.

At Pemberley next morning conversation was not easy. Georgiana was not used to being a hostess, and Bingley's sisters said little. But when the gentlemen entered, the conversation came to life.

Miss Bingley then let loose her feelings.

"I hear, Miss Eliza, that Colonel Forster's regiment has left. That must be a great loss for *your* family."

She dared not mention Wickham's name, but Elizabeth

understood her meaning. She answered calmly. But Miss Darcy was not so calm. She, too, had understood the unspoken name, and was upset. Miss Bingley knew nothing of Wickham's connection with Georgiana.

After Elizabeth and her aunt had gone, she said more. "It's amazing that she was thought to be a beauty in Meryton," she said to Darcy. "I believe even you thought her pretty once."

"Yes," said Darcy, after remaining silent through several similar remarks, "and now I think she is the most attractive woman I have ever met."

Meanwhile, Elizabeth returned to the inn and found a letter from Jane. It contained the most worrying news. Colonel Forster had written to say that Lydia had run away – with Wickham. It was first thought that they had gone to Scotland to get married. But Colonel Forster, after trying to follow their movements, thought they were still in London. Mr Bennet had gone to London and needed Mr Gardiner's help. Elizabeth jumped up and ran to the door to find her uncle. But just as she reached it, a servant opened it and Darcy appeared.

"Good heavens!" he exclaimed. "What's the matter?"

She sent the servant to fetch her uncle and burst into tears. It was some minutes before she recovered enough to tell him what had happened.

"I might have prevented it," she said. "If only I'd told my family what I knew about his character!"

Darcy hardly seemed to hear. He walked about deep in thought until Mr Gardiner appeared, then he left. Elizabeth wept again. Lydia had destroyed her hopes of Darcy's love and respect for ever.

Chapter 13
A wedding

They travelled fast, reaching Longbourn by dinner-time the next day. Mrs Bennet received them as might be expected: with tears, wild attacks against Wickham, but mostly with complaints about her own sufferings. Mr Gardiner told her not to get alarmed. He would go straight to London, he said, and talk to Mr Bennet.

"Just find them," said Mrs Bennet, "and if they're not married, make them get married. Don't wait for wedding-clothes. Tell Lydia she can have as much money as she likes to buy them after the wedding. And above all, keep Mr Bennet from fighting. Tell him what a terrible state I'm in – pains in my side, headaches, and such a beating of my heart that I can't sleep."

The Gardiners left next morning, and from then the Bennets could only wait for news. Mrs Philips called sometimes "to give them comfort", as she said. But since she never came without fresh stories of Wickham's unpaid debts, she always left them feeling worse.

A letter from Mr Collins contained the same kind of comfort. Lydia, he kindly pointed out, would be better dead than living in her present state. However, her parents must not think themselves wholly to blame, for Lydia must have been bad by nature. He said he pitied them. Lady Catherine, to whom he had told the news, also pitied them. "She agrees with me that this fault in one daughter will harm the chances in marriage of the others. How lucky I am to have escaped a closer connection with your family last November!"

Mr Bennet finally returned, but with no news of the

missing pair. His wife was not too pleased.

"What! Have you come home without Lydia?" she cried. "Who is now to fight Wickham and make him marry her?"

Then two days later came another letter from Mr Gardiner with better news. Lydia and Wickham had been found. "They are not married," he wrote, "but if you do what I have promised for you, they will be. All you have to do is agree to pay Lydia £100 a year."

He went on to say that Wickham's situation was not as bad as they had believed. When all his debts had been paid there would be enough money left to buy him a place in another regiment at present in the north of England. He advised Mr Bennet to stay at Longbourn. Lydia would be married from his house in London.

"So you'll agree to this," said Elizabeth.

"I must," her father said. "There are only two things I want to know: first, how much money your uncle has paid Wickham, and secondly, how I am ever going to repay your uncle."

"Money!" cried Jane, "whatever do you mean?"

"I mean that no man of any sense would marry Lydia for £100 a year. Wickham's a fool if he takes her for a penny less than £10,000. I can't repay half that."

"I can't believe our uncle can spare so much money," said Elizabeth. "He has children of his own."

But no thoughts of money entered Mrs Bennet's head when they told her the news.

"My dear, dear Lydia!" she cried. "This is delightful news! She's going to be married! – I shall see her again! – She'll be married at sixteen! – My good, kind brother! – I knew he would manage everything! – How I long to see her and my dear Wickham too!"

The news of the coming marriage spread quickly through the neighbourhood. It would have been more interesting if Lydia had *not* got married. But even as it was, there was plenty for all the old ladies to talk about.

Mrs Bennet was now thinking of a house for Lydia.

"Haye Park might do, if only the Gouldings would leave, or the great house at Stoke, if the sitting room was not so small. But Ashworth is too far off."

Mr Bennet let her run on until the servants had left the room, then said: "Before you choose a house for your daughter, Mrs Bennet, let this be understood. There is one house in this neighbourhood where they will not be received, and that is Longbourn."

That was Mrs Bennet's first shock. The second was when he told her he would not give a penny for new clothes for Lydia. She could not understand. Not to have new clothes for a wedding was more shameful than running away and living with Wickham for two weeks.

The wedding day arrived. In spite of his hard words, Mr Bennet had been persuaded by Jane to let the Wickhams come on to Longbourn from London, and stay a few days before going north to join his regiment.

Their reception at Longbourn was mixed. Mr Bennet was very cool, while his wife was full of joy. As for Lydia, she showed no shame for the trouble she had caused. All she could think of was her new position as a married woman: showing off her ring to the servants, and claiming a more important seat at the dining-table. Wickham, too, was perfectly at his ease.

While the Wickhams stayed, Elizabeth tried to avoid them as much as possible. Perhaps that was why she failed to hear Lydia's description of her wedding. But her sister could not bear that anyone should not hear her story, and finding Elizabeth alone one day, told her every-thing. Elizabeth sat there half listening, until Lydia suddenly said something very interesting.

"My uncle was so late coming to take us to the church," she said, "that I got quite frightened that he wouldn't come at all. But then I thought, Mr Darcy could always give me away —"

"Mr Darcy!" cried Elizabeth. "Was he there, then?"

"Why yes – with Wickham, you know. But I quite forgot. That was a secret, and I promised not to say."

"If it was a secret you need say no more," said Elizabeth, but she could not leave Darcy's presence at the wedding unexplained. She wrote to her aunt.

In her reply Mrs Gardiner said she thought Elizabeth already knew everything from Darcy. That was why her husband had agreed to do what he had done. Darcy had discovered the pair at the house of Mrs Young, who after leaving his employment had lived by letting rooms. Wickham was still hoping for a richer wife, but he had no money·and no job. In the end he had to accept Darcy's conditions. These were that he would pay Wickham's debts and buy him a place in another regiment, if Wickham married Lydia.

Darcy had then told Mr Gardiner what he had arranged. He said he did not want it to be known that he had given money to Wickham. He wanted it to appear that Mr Gardiner had done so. Mr Gardiner had not liked this arrangement, but Darcy had forced him to agree.

Elizabeth sighed. What did Darcy mean by all this: to take this trouble for a girl like Lydia; to meet and discuss with the man he most wished to avoid? How much she wished for his respect! But it was too late now.

Chapter 14
A return

The departure of Lydia was a sad event for Mrs Bennet. But she was not to be unhappy for long. Good news was on the way. The housekeeper at Netherfield had received orders to prepare the house for her master.

While her mother excitedly began to plan dinners, Jane felt only anxiety and alarm. She did not dare to hope and risk another disappointment.

"As soon as Mr Bingley arrives at Netherfield," said Mrs Bennet to her husband, "you *must* call on him."

"You made me call on him last year, promising he would marry one of my daughters. But it all ended in nothing. I shan't waste my time again," he replied.

She then said that she would ask him to dinner whether Mr Bennet called or not. However, before she could do this, and only two days after his arrival at Netherfield, Bingley was seen riding towards the house – but not alone. Catherine, shouted from the window:

"There's a gentleman with him, Mama. It's that man who used to be with him before – that tall, proud man."

"Goodness!" said her mother. "Mr Darcy – so it is! Well, any friend of Mr Bingley is welcome here, but I must say that I hate the sight of him."

She received Bingley with great friendliness. Too much friendliness, Elizabeth felt, compared with the cold politeness of her welcome to Darcy. Bingley himself appeared pleased, but at the same time, uneasy.

"We were afraid you'd never come back again," said Mrs Bennet. "There have been changes since you left. Miss Lucas is married, and so is one of our daughters. It was in the papers, but it wasn't put in properly – nothing about her family or where she lived. I don't know how my brother came to make such a mistake."

While Bingley gave his good wishes, Elizabeth did not dare lift up her eyes to see how Darcy looked.

"Her husband has now joined another regiment," Mrs Bennet went on. "It shows he has *some* friends."

As this was directed at Darcy, Elizabeth's misery and shame increased. In fact this visit, and a dinner the following night for the two gentlemen, gave her no joy at all. Darcy hardly said anything, and was not as natural and at his ease as he had been at Pemberley.

"If he comes here only to be silent," she complained to Jane, "why does he come at all?"

Meanwhile, Mrs Bennet thought only of trying to leave Jane and Bingley alone together. After Mr Bennet had gone off as usual to his library, she would sit looking hard at her other daughters as a sign to make them leave the room. But Catherine often did not understand these signs and would ask her mother what she wanted, while Elizabeth took no notice of them.

In any case Bingley refused to be hurried. He wanted to choose his own time and place. But in the end he did indeed ask Jane to be his wife.

Jane's feelings do not need to be described. As for her mother, Lydia and Wickham were quite forgotten. Jane was now her favourite child. Mr Bennet, too, was in his own way delighted.

"I'm sure you'll be very happy," he said. "Each of you thinks so much of the feelings of the other that you'll never agree on anything. You're so kind-hearted that every servant will cheat you, and so ready to give that you'll never have enough money."

Chapter 15
An unexpected visit

One morning, a week after Bingley asked Jane to marry him, a large carriage drawn by four horses stopped outside the house. It was too grand for any of the neighbours. So the ladies were prepared to be surprised when the door opened and their visitor was shown in. It was Lady Catherine de Bourgh.

Elizabeth introduced her mother, and Lady Catherine gave her a nod. "You have a very small park here," she said.

"It's nothing to compare with Rosings, I dare say, my Lady," said Mrs Bennet, "but it's much larger than Sir William Lucas's."

After more remarks like this from Lady Catherine, silence fell. Then, turning to Elizabeth, she said:

"I should be glad to take a walk in your grounds, if you would give me the favour of your company."

"Go, my dear," cried Mrs Bennet, "and show Lady Catherine everything. I'm sure she'll enjoy the rose garden."

It soon became clear, however, that enjoyment was not the purpose of Lady Catherine's visit. "I'm quite sure you know the reason for my visit here," she said.

"Why, no," said Elizabeth in surprise.

"Miss Bennet, although you may choose to be insincere, I do not. Let me come to the point. A most alarming report has come to my ears. I hear that you have hopes of marrying my nephew, Mr Darcy. This cannot, of course, be true."

"If you know this story to be untrue, why did you

come so far to tell it to me?" Elizabeth asked.

"To make sure that the report is publicly denied."

"But by coming here you're likely to make the report more widely believed – if such a report exists."

"Miss Bennet, I must have an answer. Has my nephew made you an offer of marriage or not?"

"If he has," said Elizabeth, "I shan't tell you."

"Understand this. Such a marriage can never take place. Mr Darcy is to marry my daughter."

"If that is so, you need have no fear that he would ask to marry me," said Elizabeth.

Lady Catherine paused a moment, then replied: "The arrangement between them is of a special kind. They were intended for each other from childhood. It was my wish, and his mother's. These wishes are not now to be upset by a young woman like you. So tell me, is there, or is there not, an agreement between you?"

"No."

Lady Catherine looked more pleased. "And do you promise never to enter into such an agreement?"

"I shall make no such promise," said Elizabeth.

Lady Catherine then turned her full anger on her. She raged on about Lydia's marriage, honour, duty, and ungrateful behaviour until she reached the door of her carriage. She then drove off without even going inside to say goodbye to Mrs Bennet.

Where had this story come from? From the Collinses Elizabeth supposed. But what could Lady Catherine hope to gain from this extraordinary visit?

Next morning the affair came up again when her father approached with a letter in his hand. "I'd like you to read this," he said. "It amuses me a great deal. I didn't know I had two daughters about to marry."

Elizabeth's face reddened. Could it be from Darcy? Surely he would not write to her father before speaking to her.

"You'll be surprised when you hear of your admirer," her father went on. "The letter is from Mr Collins. I shan't waste time on his good wishes to Jane and Mr Bingley, but listen to this:

'Your daughter Elizabeth may not long remain unmarried. The young gentleman who admires her has every advantage as a husband – and yet, let me warn my cousin. We believe that his aunt, Lady Catherine, does not look on this affair with a friendly eye.'

"So, my dear," said Mr Bennet. "Mr Darcy is your man. Could there be anyone less likely? Mr Darcy, who never looks at any woman except to find a fault – who probably never looked at you at all. Really, I wouldn't give up Mr Collins's letters for anything."

He laughed. But Elizabeth felt more like crying. Her father was wrong to think that Darcy had so little interest in her. But was he *so* wrong? If he had still been interested he would have spoken by now.

Bingley was now a daily visitor to Longbourn, where he spent the mornings with Jane. But one day, a week after Lady Catherine's visit, two horsemen appeared.

"Why!" cried Mrs Bennet. "Here's that unpleasant Mr Darcy again with dear Bingley. I'm sorry, Lizzy, but I think you'll have to talk to him today."

It seemed a good idea for all four of them to go for a walk. So they set off two by two along the lane. Elizabeth and Darcy went faster than Jane and Bingley, and quite soon they were some way ahead. This was the first time since Pemberley that they had been alone together, and

Elizabeth could not wait to say what she knew of Darcy's part in Lydia's marriage. But when she tried to express her family's thanks, he stopped her.

"Don't talk of your family," he said. "Whatever I did, I did for you alone."

Elizabeth's eyes filled with tears. She could not speak, so Darcy continued: "You're too kind to make me suffer any longer. My feelings for you haven't changed since Hunsford. Though I'm still ashamed of how I expressed them. But if yours are still unchanged, just say, and I'll be silent for ever."

Elizabeth explained that her feelings *had* changed. They had changed a great deal. So Darcy did not have to be silent. Indeed, far from being silent he went on to express his feelings very fully. These would not have pleased his aunt, but they pleased Elizabeth more than anything had ever pleased her before.

He also explained why he had decided to risk a second refusal. On her way through London his aunt had called and tried to make him promise not to marry her. It was this which had encouraged him to return.

They walked for two hours without knowing where they had been. Then as soon as they returned, Darcy went straight to see Mr Bennet. It was some time before he re-appeared and asked Elizabeth to go to her father.

Mr Bennet looked serious. "Lizzy," he said, "are you determined to accept this man? I always understood that you hated him."

It was not easy to persuade him that her feelings *had* changed, and that it was Darcy she loved, not Pemberley or £10,000 a year. She also told him about the part Darcy had played in Lydia's marriage.

"If it had been your uncle's doing," he said, "I should

have had to pay the money back. But these violent lovers always want their own way. I'll offer to pay him tomorrow, but I know he'll talk wildly about how much he loves you, and that will be the end of it."

When Mrs Bennet heard the news she was for a time quite unable to say anything. She got up, sat down again and when she spoke could only say:

"Goodness me! Lord bless me! Dear me! Mr Darcy! Who would have thought it? And is it really true? Oh my sweetest Lizzy! How rich you'll be! What jewels, what carriages you'll have! Jane's is nothing to it – nothing at all! Such a charming man! Oh Lord!"

What is left to say? Elizabeth and Jane were married, and Bingley bought a property in Derbyshire close enough to Pemberley for the sisters to visit. Catherine, warned by the example of Lydia, improved.

Lydia's story was less happy. Never settled, always short of money, she depended on help from her sisters. Wickham never gave up hope that Darcy would some day make his fortune for him. At the same time he continued to blame him for all his troubles.

The letter that Lady Catherine sent to Darcy on his marriage was so insulting to Elizabeth, that for a long time he refused to have anything to do with her. In the end, however, Elizabeth persuaded him to forget his anger and Lady Catherine was received at Pemberley.

As for Mr and Mrs Gardiner, their wish to re-visit Pemberley was granted many times over, for they were regular and ever-welcome guests.

Questions

Questions on each chapter

1
  1 Who was "single, rich and young"?
  2 What did Mrs Bennet hope?
  3 What did Mr Bennet do the next morning?
  4 Why did Mrs Bennet visit Lady Lucas?

2
  1 Why would Longbourn pass to Mr Bennet's cousin?
  2 Why did everyone like Mr Bingley?
  3 How did Mr Darcy upset Elizabeth?
  4 Describe Charlotte Lucas.

3
  1 Why did the Bingley sisters invite Jane to dinner?
  2 Why couldn't Jane go to Netherfield by carriage?
  3 What did the Bingley sisters think of the Bennets?
  4 Who was Darcy writing to?
  5 What fault did Darcy admit to having?

4
  1 What was Mr Bennet's surprise?
  2 What is the reason Mr Collins gives in his letter for visiting the Bennets? (He wanted . . .)
  3 What was Mr Collins's favourite subject of conversation?
  4 What did Mr Bennet think of Mr Collins?

5
  1 Why had Mr Collins really come to Longbourn?
  2 Who was Mrs Philips, and where did she live?
  3 How did Wickham know Darcy?
  4 How were Darcy and Lady Catherine connected?
  5 Why was Elizabeth looking forward to the dance?

6
  1 Why was Elizabeth disappointed?
  2 In what way was Mr Collins a bad dancer?
  3 What did Mr Collins discover at the dance?
  4 How did Darcy treat Mr Collins?
  5 Why did Mrs Bennet leave the dance feeling happy?

7 1 Why was Mr Collins trying to get married?
  2 What did Mrs Bennet want her husband to do?
  3 What did Mr Bennet want Elizabeth to do?
  4 Why did Mr Collins visit the Lucases?

8 1 Where did the Bingleys go?
  2 How did Miss Bingley's letters affect Jane?
  3 Who was Mr Gardiner?
  4 How did Mrs Gardiner try to help Jane?
  5 Why did Mrs Gardiner advise Elizabeth not to fall in love with Wickham?

9 1 Describe Mr Collins's behaviour before they left to go to Rosings.
  2 How did he behave during dinner?
  3 Who was Colonel Fitzwilliam?
  4 What did Charlotte think of Darcy's call on Elizabeth?

10 1 What did Elizabeth learn from Fitzwilliam?
  2 Why did Darcy call on Elizabeth a second time?
  3 What was his reason for separating Jane and Bingley?
  4 What was old Mr Darcy's plan for Wickham?
  5 How did Elizabeth feel after reading Darcy's letter?

11 1 Who met Elizabeth and Maria on their way home?
  2 What news did Lydia have about Wickham?
  3 Why were Lydia and Catherine unhappy?
  4 Where did Lydia want to go?
  5 Why couldn't the Gardiners go to the Lakes?

12 1 Why didn't Elizabeth want to visit Pemberley?
  2 How did the housekeeper surprise her?
  3 What happened after they left the house?
  4 How did the Gardiners recognise Darcy?
  5 What did they think about Darcy's behaviour?
  6 What was Jane's bad news?

13 1 Where was Mr Bennet, and what was he doing?
  2 What did Mr Gardiner ask Mr Bennet to agree to?
  3 Where did Lydia's marriage take place?
  4 Why did Mr Bennet let the Wickhams visit Longbourn?
  5 How did Lydia behave?
  6 What was the secret that Elizabeth learnt?

14 1 What was the good news that Mrs Bennet heard?
2 Why did she try to leave Bingley and Jane alone?

15 1 Why did Lady Catherine visit Longbourn?
2 Who sent Mr Bennet a letter?
3 What made Darcy ask Elizabeth again to marry him?
4 Where did Jane and Bingley go and live? Why?

Questions on the whole story

These are harder questions. Read the Introduction, and think hard about the questions before you answer them. Some of them ask for your opinion, and there is no fixed answer.

1 Do you think Mr Bennet was a good father?

2 What do you think about Charlotte's decision to marry Mr Collins? Was it a good marriage?

3 Why, do you think, did Elizabeth believe in Wickham for so long?

4 What events made Elizabeth change her mind about Darcy?

5 Describe the character of Jane. Do you admire her?

6 Describe Lydia's behaviour to
a her parents; b her sisters

7 What mistakes did Miss Bingley make in trying to attract Darcy?

8 What mistakes did Mrs Bennet make in trying to get Jane married to Bingley?

9 Was Mrs Bennet a suitable wife for Mr Bennet?

10 In what ways was Lady Catherine rude and bad-mannered?

11 Elizabeth is called many things in this book. Who calls her
a Lizzy; b Miss Bennet; c Miss Eliza Bennet or Miss Eliza?

New words

colonel
an officer in charge of a
regiment

regiment
a group of 600 to 1,000
soldiers

parson
a minister of the Church of
England

prejudice
forming an opinion before
one has knowledge of a
person or thing